THE MESSAGE
BOOK 2 DARK WATER

PJ GRAY

SADDLEBACK
EDUCATIONAL PUBLISHING

THE MESSAGE
BOOK 2 DARK WATER

SADDLEBACK
EDUCATIONAL PUBLISHING
www.sdlback.com

All source images from Shutterstock.com

ISBN-13: 978-1-68021-150-4
ISBN-10: 1-68021-150-1
eBook: 978-1-63078-482-9

Printed in Malaysia

21 20 19 18 17   3 4 5 6 7

AUTHOR ACKNOWLEDGEMENTS

I wish to thank Carol Senderowitz for her friendship and belief in my abilities. Additional thanks and gratitude to my family and friends for their love and support; likewise to the staff at Saddleback Educational Publishing for their generosity, graciousness, and enthusiasm. Most importantly, my heartfelt thanks to Scott Drawe for his love and support.

MISSING

Dakota "Dack" Peck was in big trouble.

Dack had some strange dreams. The dreams made no sense. They led him to Mrs. Miller's house. Mrs. Miller was his math teacher last year.

Dack broke into the Millers' house. He had to find answers. The dreams were too real. Tim Ward was his friend. He had been missing for a while. Tim visited Dack in his dreams.

Dack knew Tim took drugs. Tim was in trouble. Dack just knew it.

"I know some stuff," Tim said. "It will blow this town up. I'm going to the press, man."

That was the last day Dack saw Tim. Then Tim went missing. His new car was found. He was not in it. The police could not find him.

Mrs. Miller's husband was a local cop. "He's on that case," she had said.

Dack stood in the Millers' home. His dreams had brought him here. He was looking for clues. Something. Anything.

But what? He kept thinking of his dreams. The number 1-1-5-5. Water. Mrs. Miller's house. Were these clues?

Then he heard a sound. Voices?

The front door!

Someone was coming.

OPEN WINDOW

The front door opened. Mr. and Mrs. Miller were home.

Dack was in their kitchen. He could hear them.

His heart was racing. Where could he hide? He looked for a way out. The kitchen window was open. Just a crack. He opened it wider.

Dack climbed out the window. Fell to the ground. He was in an alley. Where could he go? The other houses were close. He hid behind trash cans.

Dack heard Mr. Miller at the window. Run! Now! But he did not. He held his breath. And waited. He could hear the Millers inside.

Mr. Miller stood near the window. "Did you leave the window open?" he asked.

"No," Mrs. Miller said. "I don't think so."

"You always forget to close it."

"That's not true."

"Are you calling me a liar?" Mr. Miller asked.

Smack!

Mrs. Miller screamed. There was a crash. Then yelling.

Mr. Miller hit his wife again.

Dack froze. He wanted to run. But he would be seen. The window was still open. He was mad. He liked Mrs. Miller. He did not want her to get hurt.

Dack looked down. Saw some weeds.
Then saw something else. A small card. It
was cut. He picked it up. Looked closer.
It was part of an ID. Most of it was gone.
But not the photo.

It was Tim Ward! It was his photo. Dack's eyes grew wide. He was in shock. This was Tim's ID. How did it get here?

Slam!

The kitchen window slammed shut. Dack froze. Then he heard someone in the alley. A back door closed. Then a dog barked. He knew he had to run. Dack put the photo in his pocket.

He ran. Fast. Then got to his truck. And drove away.

WHITE DEER

Dack tried to sleep that night. He tossed.
And turned. His mind took him back. To
the Millers' house. To the close call with
Mr. Miller.

He held Tim's ID. It was only a piece. But
it was a clue. Why was it near the Millers'
trash cans? Why was it cut?

He wanted to dream again. He needed more clues. The clues could help. Help to find Tim.

Dack heard his mom. She was in the kitchen. He should tell her about the dreams. What would she say?

Dack got out of bed. He went into the kitchen.

His mom sat at the table. There were papers from work on it. And a handgun. She was cleaning it. Dack was surprised.

"Mom?" he asked. He rubbed his eyes. "What are you doing with that?"

"Don't worry," she said. "It's legal."

"You never told me you had a gun."

"I know," she said. "I should have."

"But why?" he asked.

"I feel better having it," she said. "I sell houses. Drive a lot. I'm out there alone. I feel better having it with me."

Dack's mom loaded the gun. "I never told you this," she said. "But I wanted to be a cop."

"What?" Dack said. "When?"

"When you were a baby," she said. "Your dad was not happy about it. He hated the idea. So I didn't do it."

"You would have been a great cop," Dack said.

She smiled. "I think so too," she said. "My dad taught me how to shoot. How to be safe with guns. Did I ever tell you that?"

Dack smiled. Shook his head.

"Why are you awake?" she asked.

"I can't sleep," he said.

"Do you want to talk about it?"

"About what?" he asked. He would not look at her.

"About what's on your mind."

Dack was silent.

"Is it about your friend Tim?"

Dack looked up. He did not know what to say.

"I know it's been hard," she said. "He's still missing. You feel helpless. Am I right?"

"Yes," he said.

"We all do," she said, shaking her head. "I don't get it. What are the police doing? We haven't heard anything. Nothing on the news."

"What do you think about dreams?" Dack asked.

"Dreams? Well, dreams can mean many things. Some mean nothing," she said. "Some dreams are powerful."

"Powerful?" Dack asked. "How?"

"Our people believe in the power of dreams. Your grandfather did. He was a healer. A great man. Many in our tribe came to him. For advice. For help. You are named after him."

"I know," Dack said. "I wish I'd met him."

"So do I," she said. "He once told me a story. The story of the white deer. The white deer is a dream spirit. It's holy to us."

"Did he see one in a dream?" Dack asked.

"Yes," she said. "It is a powerful sign. It means something big will happen. It helps you. Guides you to where you need to go." She looked at Dack. "Did you dream of a white deer?"

"No, Mom," he said.

She stood up. Looked at the clock. "It's very late," she said. "We both need some sleep." She kissed his head. Then passed him. Stopped and turned. "Before I forget," she said. "Did you see my phone?"

"No," he said. "Why?"

She took a phone out of her bag. Handed it to Dack. "You left this on the table." It was Dack's cell phone. "Our phones look the same," she said. "I keep picking yours up by mistake."

Dack smiled.

"Good night," she said. "I love you." She walked out of the kitchen.

WINNING NUMBERS

Dack went back to bed. He was glad his mom was up. Glad he had talked to her.

He grew tired. His eyes got heavy. Soon he fell asleep.

Dack did not dream of the white deer. But he did dream. Dack was in Tim's house. Tim was wearing his lucky red shirt. They were watching a big TV.

"Be quiet!" Tim shouted. "It's coming. It's coming."

"What's coming?" Dack asked.

"The winning numbers," Tim said.

Numbers flashed on the TV. Music played.

A voice said, "Today's winning numbers. Are you ready? 1 … 1 … 5 … 5."

Tim jumped up. "I won! I won!" he yelled.

"Wait," Dack said. "How? What's going on? What did you win?"

"Look!" Tim said. He pointed to the TV.

The voice said, "The winner gets a cabin. It's brand new."

Tim jumped up and down. "Did you hear that?" Tim asked. "I won a cabin!"

A picture came on the screen. There was a small log cabin. It was in a forest. A large river flowed behind it. A small bridge went over the river.

"I won! I won!" Tim said again. "I won a cabin!"

Dack shook his head. "I don't get it," he said. "Why do you want a cabin?" He looked at Tim. "Are you bleeding?" Dack saw blood. "Tim? What's going on? Your mouth. It's bleeding!"

Then Dack looked down. The floor was wet. Water poured into the house. The windows cracked. Water came in through the cracks.

Dack grabbed Tim's arm. "We have to go!" he yelled. "Come on! We have to get out of here."

Tim watched the TV. He did not look at Dack.

"Didn't you hear me?" Dack asked. "Hurry!" He pulled Tim's arm.

Water flooded the room. Tim did not seem to care.

"Hurry!" Dack yelled. "We have to get out!"

Dack sat up in his bed. "Get out!" he yelled out loud. Then he woke up. His heart was racing. He tried to catch his breath. He was wet. Wet with sweat.

Dack fell back onto his pillow. He could not go back to sleep.

DAY OFF

Two days passed. Dack had not dreamed of Tim.

He still had Tim's ID. Just the one piece. It was in his wallet.

He sat in the kitchen. What could he do? Go to the police? Show them Tim's card? Tell them how he found it? What about Mr. Miller? He was the cop on the case.

Dack kept thinking. Did Tim go to the Millers' house? Why?

Dack's mom walked in. She was in a hurry. She got some coffee. "You're up early," she said. "Do you work today?"

"No," he said. "I have the day off."

Dack's mom grabbed her purse. "Day off?" she asked. "Good! Then you have time to clean."

"What?"

"You heard me," she said. "Clean your bedroom. Clean your bathroom. And do your other chores."

Dack smiled. "Okay," he said.

His mom got her car keys and phone. "I'll miss dinner tonight," she said. "I have to work late." She opened the door. Turned around. Looked at Dack. "There's plenty of food," she said. "See you later. Love you!" Then she left.

Dack smiled. Shook his head.

The door opened. His mom looked at him.

"Forget something?" he asked.

"Yes," she said. "Did you ever talk to Mrs. Miller?"

Dack turned cold. "What?"

"Her lake house. On Black Lake. Will she sell it?"

Dack shook his head.

"Did you see her at work?" she asked. "I asked you to ask her."

"No," he said. "I haven't seen her lately."

"Please, ask her if you see her. I know someone. They want to buy a house on Black Lake. There are very few houses out there."

Dack nodded his head.

"Thanks!" she said. She left again.

Dack sat still. Then it came to him. The dream. The cabin. The river. The bridge. Could the Millers' lake house be a clue?

He had to find out.

Dack grabbed his wallet and car keys. He looked for his phone. It had been on the table. Now it was gone. His mom! She must have picked it up.

Now he had no phone. So what? Not a big deal.

He had to get to the Millers' lake house.

ON THE ROAD

Dack drove his truck. He headed to the Millers' lake house.

His mind took him back. "At the end of Old Pine Road," his mom had said. That was all Dack knew.

He drove out of town. His gas tank was low. Where was the closest station? He looked. There was a small store. It had a gas pump.

Dack filled the tank. He paid inside the store.

An old man worked behind the counter. "I think I know you," the man said.

"I don't think so," Dack said. "I'm not from around here."

"Yes," the man said. "You're Mrs. Peck's boy. You look like her."

"How do you know my mom?"

"It's been a few years," he said. "I'm Jim Cook."

They shook hands.

"Your mom helped me sell some land. She came by my old place. You were with her."

Dack did not recall.

"How is your mom?" he asked.

"She's good." Dack wanted to leave. Fast! He did not want to talk.

"Well, give your mom my best."

"I will," Dack said. "Thanks."

Dack left. Then got back into his truck. He took off. "Everybody knows Mom," he said to himself. Could his mom be nearby? She could be working anywhere.

Dack kept driving. He drove to the nearby forest. Near Black Lake. What would he find? He did not know. He just had to go there.

A sign said *Old Pine Road*. He was deep in the woods. Black Lake was close. He saw no houses. No people.

He kept driving. There was one house. He saw it through the trees. He saw a driveway. There were no cars. He pulled over. Parked behind some trees.

Dack walked up the driveway. The trees were thick. It was hard to see the sun. He got closer to the house. There was a sign. Near the front door.

The Millers

This was it.

LAKE HOUSE

Dack walked slowly around back. No one was home. He felt sick. His stomach turned.

There was a large backyard. Then the edge of Black Lake.

Dack saw a long dock. It looked old. Broken. And a little creepy. He could not stop staring at it. He had to get closer.

Dack walked through the backyard. He got to the water's edge.

The sun felt warm on his face. The water looked black. Even on a sunny day. Black Lake. Now it made sense.

He looked down the old dock. And saw a thick rope. It was tied around a post. The end of the rope fell into the water. Why was it there? There was no boat.

He had to find out.

He took his first step onto the dock. Then looked down. The water was not deep. Something flashed in the water. What was it? Something small. Shiny.

Dack reached into the lake. Touched something cold. Hard. A piece of metal. He lifted it out. Rubbed it clean. It was a police badge.

He felt sick. His hand began to shake.

The badge number was 1-1-5-5.

DARK WATER

Dack held the badge in his hand. The badge number. The same number from his dreams. Was this Mr. Miller's badge?

He looked down the dock. Saw the rope. He had to get there.

Dack walked on. There were missing boards. He stepped with care.

He made it to the end. Reached down. Grabbed the rope. Pulled hard. There was something in the water. Something heavy.

He pulled harder. A big black bag. It was tied to the rope. He pulled again. Grabbed the bag. Lifted it onto the dock.

Water splashed. The bag was tied with heavy tape. He tore a hole. Opened the bag a little. And froze. Wet hair. Blue skin.

It was a body.

Wet hair. An ear. Then a neck. The top of a shirt. It was red. At that moment Dack knew. It was Tim's lucky red shirt.

This was Tim.

Dack fell onto the dock. He put his hands to his face. Shook his head. "Why Tim?" he said. "How? How did this happen?"

"Dack Peck?" a voice called out. "Is that you?"

It was Mrs. Miller.

ABOUT THE AUTHOR

PJ Gray is a versatile, award-winning freelance writer experienced in short stories, essays, and feature writing. He is a former managing editor for *Pride* magazine, a ghost writer, blogger, researcher, food writer, and cookbook author. He currently resides in Chicago, Illinois. For more information about PJ Gray, go to www.pjgray.com.